TRUMPETS WEST!

TRUMPETS WEST!

LUKE SHORT

INTRODUCTION BY
JOHN BETANCOURT

WILDSIDE PRESS

INTRODUCTION

Luke Short (real name Frederick Dilley Glidden, Nov. 19, 1908 – Aug. 18, 1975) was a popular Western writer.

Born in Kewanee, Illinois Glidden attended the University of Illinois at Urbana-Champaign for two and a half years and then transferred to the University of Missouri at Columbia to study journalism.

Following graduation in 1930 he worked for a number of newspapers before becoming a trapper in Canada then later moved to New Mexico to be an archeologist's assistant.

After reading Western pulp magazines and trying to escape unemployment he started writing Western fiction. He sold his first short story and novel in 1935 under the pen name of Luke Short (which was also the name of a famous gunslinger in the Old West, though it's unclear if he was aware of that when he assumed the pen name.)

Short's apprenticeship in the pulps was comparatively brief. In 1938 he sold a short story, "The Warning" to *Collier's* and in 1941 he sold his novel *Blood on the Moon* aka *Gunman's Chance* to *The Saturday Evening Post*.

After publishing over a dozen novels in the 1930s, he started writing for films in the '40s. In 1948 alone four Luke Short novels appeared as movies. Some of his memorable film credits includes *Ramrod* (1947) and *Blood on the Moon* (1948).

Short's novel *The Whip* aka *Doom Cliff* was serialized in both *Collier's* and *The Saturday Evening Post*. The first two parts were published in *Collier's* in the December 21, 1956 and the January 4, 1957 issues. Collier's then ceased publication. *The Saturday Evening Post* bought the rights to the remaining unpublished installment and published it on February 9, 1957.

He continued to write novels, despite increasing trouble with his eyes, until his death in 1975. His ashes are buried in Aspen, Colorado, his home at the time of his death.

* * * *

Trumpets West! (1957) was the first volume of a line of novellas Dell published as "A Dell 10 Cent Book."

—John Betancourt
Cabin John, Maryland

CHAPTER ONE

UNDER ARREST

Fort Akin's one-room hospital stood at a corner of the parade grounds. Out of respect for the newly sown grass, those who wanted to reach headquarters building in the center of the opposite side of the ground had been ordered to use the gravel walk.

On this late afternoon of an Arizona July, however, Lieutenant Burke Hanna stepped out of the hospital door and cut string-straight across the parade ground. He was a tall, unshaven, and dirty man in a moderate hurry, and his field uniform was grimed a color closer to gray than blue.

Crossing the gravel drive, he went up the short walk of headquarters building. A hulking, barrel-chested sergeant major with a black, short-clipped beard that reached almost to his eyes, was coming down the veranda steps. He saluted and said, "Glad you're back, sir."

"Thanks, O'Mara," Burke said. His foot was on the bottom step when he halted, turned, and called, "O'Mara!"

The sergeant came back to him, and Burke said, "Did you see those ration requests I sent in by Hardy?"

"Yes, sir," O'Mara said in the bland voice of an old soldier who knows his rights. "Captain Ervien wouldn't sign them, sir."

Burke said, "Right. Thanks," and went up the steps. Standing in the big doorway of the adobe building was Lieutenant Abe Byas, a big man with a morose and homely face and so wide of shoulder that he nearly blocked the doorway—which seemed to his intention now.

Burke hauled up, and Byas said with gentle mockery in his deep voice, "Counted ten, Burke?"

"I've counted ten thousand," Burke said grimly. "Let me past, Abe."

"Sure," Byas said, not moving. The two men regarded each other a long moment, then Burke Hanna drew a deep breath.

"All right," he said patiently. He lifted off his dusty campaign hat and beat at his trousers with it. His black hair, ragged at the edges, was darker than the thick beard stubble swirled on his lean and weather-blackened face. When he looked up, his wide mouth was humorless. He said bitterly, "What's gone on here, Abe?"

Byas only shook his head in kindly refusal to answer. "Did Doc Ford see your cripples?"

Burke nodded, and said in the same bitter voice, "Two men half dead with dysentery. Raines's feet are cut to ribbons; so are Kahn's. A half-dozen others crippled up, and another dozen starved and played out or sick from a diet of horsemeat." He paused. "Now can I get past?"

Byas stood aside, and as Burke passed him he laid a hand on his arm. "Look, don't go in there that way. Get a cinch on your temper, will you?"

"Sure, sure," Burke said wryly and went across the bare room and said to the sergeant behind the desk, "Lieutenant Hanna to see Captain Ervien."

"He's got the agent with him, Lieutenant, but he's expecting you," said the sergeant.

"Yes," Burke said dryly. He paced once across the room and caught sight of Byas, huge in the doorway, watching him gloomily. Byas said, "Calla says come over for dinner tonight."

Burke said, "All right, thanks," in as polite a voice as he could muster, then turned and looked speculatively at one of the chairs as Byas went out. If he sat down he would never want to get up, he knew.

The door in the wall ahead of him opened, and a big, soft, pale man in an oversize black suit stepped through, closing the door behind him. He and Burke saw each other at the same time. For an instant it seemed as if there would be no recognition, then Burke said idly, "Hello, Corinne."

The Apache agent smiled and said with a false heartiness, "How are you, Hanna?" He nodded courteously to the sergeant and went out.

Burke crushed his dusty campaign hat under his left arm, knocked firmly on the door Corinne had just closed, opened it, and went inside.

Captain Ervien was at his desk, which was set across the corner of the room between two windows. The American flag and the squadron standard were stacked behind him. He did not look up until Burke was almost in front of him.

Burke came to attention, saluted, and said, "Lieutenant Hanna reporting, sir."

Ervien returned the salute, then leaned back in his chair, regarding Burke's appearance with a dark and cynical amusement that Burke, from three years of service with him as a junior officer, knew was sincere. Whatever ease there had been between the two men had vanished long before Ervien, upon Major Drummond's death, had been appointed commanding officer. Ervien, handsome, thirty-five, with his well-tailored uniforms and his thorough and calculating knowledge of Army ways, had elected the course of the garrison soldier. Burke saw his nostrils twitch faintly, and he thought, He's smelling horse for a change.

Ervien said, "Burke, I saw you bring in K Troop. The lot of you looked more like a bunch of Mexican army deserters than soldiers."

"Maybe that's because we've been treated like Mexican deserters, Phil," Burke answered.

Ervien blandly ignored that. "You were afoot. The only officer— walking, just like a damned infantryman. Why?"

"We lost fifteen horses. Ate some, too."

"But not your own. Your sergeant was riding him."

Burke nodded shortly. "Raines had walked half the distance from Ojo Negro. His feet are badly cut. The whole troop walked half way, turn about." He added with an edge to his voice, "That's the only way we could get back here."

"You had rations and forage for five weeks," Ervien said flatly. "Enough to find that renegade Ponce and his band, fight them if you had to, send them back to the reservation, and extend your patrol. Those were your order, weren't they?"

"My dispatch to you explained that," Burke said with a mounting aggressiveness. "We shared all our supplies with Ponce and his Apaches. That's the only way we could get them back alive."

"He got to his hideout without Army rations!" Ervien flared. "Let him get back without them! Who are you to be giving away Army supplies? Let the black devils starve!"

* * * *

A blazing anger left Burke inarticulate for a moment. Ervien leaned his elbows on the desk. "Once you'd sent Ponce back, I suppose you sat there eating up your remaining rations and waiting for more instead of extending your patrol, as you were ordered?"

"We sat six days. And why not?" Burke's voice thickened with anger. "Good God, Phil, why didn't you send the forage and rations and take it out of my pay if necessary? Instead, you sent a flat refusal and ordered out the patrol!"

"You made the patrol, didn't you?"

"With half my troop afoot and sick from horsemeat!"

"You have been gone four weeks and three days." Ervien tapped he desk with his soft forefinger for emphasis. "You were issued rations for five weeks. I know that, because I just checked the supply records with Sergeant O'Mara. If you and your men suffered, you've nobody to blame but yourself."

There was, Burke knew savagely, no rebuttal open to him. Technically, Ervien was right, and yet Ponce, the Apache subchief he had been ordered to send back to the reservation, could not have brought his half-starved band through that poor, barren country without Army supplies.

Ervien leaned back, laced his fingers atop his curly chestnut hair, and surveyed Burke. He said dryly, "You feel abused, Burke?"

"I feel my men have been treated like dogs."

"Like troopers," Ervien said sharply. "And damned poorly officered troopers." He sat erect and said matter-of-factly, "We've got word that Federico, Ponce's nephew, is skulking around the Mogollon Rim north, waiting for Ponce to get fed and supplied by the agency here. When he's rested, Ponce intends to break and join him, and raid the Navajo country with him." He paused, isolating this. "Tomorrow, suppose you draw rations and forage for two weeks, take K Troop up there, confirm Federico's presence or absence, and return in two weeks. See if you can turn in a satisfactory job this time."

A stunned anger rose in Burke. He thought of his troop, a dozen hospitalized, the rest sick and exhausted, and he knew Ervien knew this. He said slowly, "You mean that, Phil?"

"Those are your orders." Ervien's lips were set grimly.

Burke had a grip on his temper, yet it was failing fast. He put both hands on Ervien's desk and leaned on them. "Phil," he began in a shaky voice, "this will make the fourth consecutive patrol for K Troop. In the past six months we've been out all but nine days. I suggest you send another troop."

"Those are your orders," Ervien repeated.

Then the rage came, and with violence. Burke slowly straightened up to attention, and said with a savage formality, "I refuse to obey them, sir."

There was a long moment of silence, during which Ervien eyed him shrewdly. Burke knew Ervien was casting up the probable results of a court martial, and when Ervien spoke now, it was still with confidence. "Want another chance, Burke?"

"No, sir," Burke said. "My only way of protesting that treatment of sick men is by refusing to obey your order. I do refuse."

Ervien said coldly, "Very well, you will consider yourself under arrest and confine your movements to the limits of the post, pending further action, Mister Hanna."

"Very good, sir." Again Burke saluted, again had it returned, about-faced, and was halfway to the door when Captain Ervien said, "By the way, Mister Hanna," in a soft, commanding voice.

Burke paused and looked at him. Ervien picked up a sheaf of papers from the corner of his desk and tapped them. "I've read your report on the alleged offenses against the Apaches committed by Mr. Alec Corinne, their agent. I've just discussed the matter with him, and have only one comment."

Burke waited silently.

"You seem to have a difficult time learning the soldiering profession. I suggest you study it and listen less to gossip. Let the Indian Bureau discipline its agents. That is not the Army's business." He tossed the paper into the wastebasket and Burke went out.

CHAPTER TWO

TENDER WELCOME

The late afternoon sunlight lay still and blazing on the parade ground, and the young trees lining the gravel walk rustled in the hot breeze. Burke tramped down the steps and turned right up the walk. The rage was still in him, a live thing that almost sickened him. He had, he knew, been systematically harried and ridden until he had rebelled—and now Ervien had him. Nor did he have to look for the reason; you didn't write blistering reports about a crooked Indian agent and submit them to a superior officer who was engaged to marry the agent's daughter, as Phil Ervien was going to marry Vinnie Corinne.

He turned up the short walk leading to the low outsize adobe building that was the unmarried officers' quarters and went in. The lounge was empty, and he went on down the corridor to his bare corner room at the rear of the building. He sank onto the plain iron bed and sat motionless, stupid with weariness.

This, then, was his homecoming—on which he had planned to be married. The prospect of seeing Calla now brought a strange reluctance to him. In a matter of minutes, Lucy, Abe's wife, would have learned of his arrest and would have told her sister Calla. News traveled like that in a remote post. And Calla, with everything set except the marriage day—which Burke was supposed to have settled with Ervien a moment ago—what would Calla do?

Tiredly, despondently, Burke pulled off his boots. She couldn't marry an officer under arrest, a man who could not wear a sword at his own wedding because he was forbidden now to carry arms, or leave the designated limits of the post. Or command troops.

Burke swore darkly, thinking, *Thirty is too damned old to let myself be baited into a fight with a CO*, but he knew that wasn't right either. Rising, he stripped off his torn and filthy uniform, put on slippers and robe, and went down the corridor to the big bathroom. There, he shaved and bathed with the slow thoroughness of a man who has done neither for many weeks, then started back to his room.

Before he reached the door, he halted and sniffed. Only one man he knew smoked the black and vile Apache trade tobacco he was smelling now. He went on, and in the doorway, before he looked, he said gloomily, "Hello, Rush, you damn carrion crow."

Rush Doll was seated back-tilted on the chair at the foot of Burke's bed, his feet on Burke's blankets. He grinned sparsely around the long cigarette pasted in the corner of his mouth. He was a man of fifty, graying and dried by decades of Arizona summers. He wore a castoff army shirt, denim pants, and Apache moccasins, and was, unqualifiedly, the best packmaster in the West, and Burke's friend.

He gibed now by way of greeting, "Footed it back, I hear."

"On horsemeat," Burke said wryly. He opened a drawer of the chest in the corner and took out some clothes.

Rush said presently, "What's a general court martial?" Burke turned to look at him.

"So it's out, is it?"

"You wouldn't go on patrol tomorrow, they say."

Burke nodded and savagely slammed the drawer shut. He said morosely, "The need for Lieutenant Hanna, and only Lieutenant Hanna, on patrol is what gravels me." He glanced obliquely at Rush. "Remember that report on Corinne you helped me with?"

Rush shook his head. "No. That's not the reason."

Something in Rush's tone held Burke motionless.

"Things have been happening since you left," Rush went on in a murmur. "He wants you out of the way."

"Things like what?"

"Your report accused Corinne of long-countin' the 'Paches so he could put their rations in his pocket, didn't it? Well, he's quit that. For the past month he's been busy tradin' the fat government-issue beef for all the scrub-cull beef anyone brings him. He trades at the rate of two fat beef for three culls."

Burke sat down slowly on his bed. "To issue to the Indians? That won't do him any good. The beef is issued to the Apaches by weight, not by count."

"What if he's rigged the agency scales to weigh out every beef at six hundred pounds or over, even if it really weighs three hundred?"

Burke only stared at him and Rush went on, "Say he gets three hundred fat beef for issue. He trades two hundred of 'em off for three hundred culls. He issues the three hundred culls weighed on his rigged scale, then sells the hundred fat ones left and pockets the money."

Burke stared down at his bare and bruised feet. Ervien's order made sense now. There was only one man in either post or agency who cared enough about the Indians' welfare to keep their agent honest, and that man was himself. And his reason was simple enough; he was tired of seeing Apaches starved into breaking out, and then having to fight or capture them. Now Ervien, protecting his prospective father-in-law, wanted him out of the way, and he had him out of the way.

As Burke reached for his socks, a thought came to him. He asked Rush, "What about Ponce's bunch I sent back? Have they been fed well and issued rations?"

"They ain't had a square meal since they hit the reservation," Rush said.

Broodingly, Burke dressed, silent now. He had almost forgotten Rush when Rush said searchingly, "You goin' to put that in your new report?"

Burke said unsmilingly, "You think Ponce would talk with me tonight?"

"How?" Rush asked. "You can't leave the post, and he ain't allowed to come on it after dark."

Burke thought a moment and said, "You bring him over to the blacksmith shop after dark. That's post limits. We can talk there and neither of us will be disobeying orders." He looked levelly at Rush. "I promised Ponce we'd treat him right if he came back. If we don't, he'll bust out and gut this country. And," he added slowly, "I wouldn't blame him."

Rush agreed and left. Burke hurriedly dressed. As he was struggling into his blouse, Lieutenants Umberhine and Cavanaugh poked their heads in to say hello. They made no reference to his arrest. Finished dressing, Burke picked up his garrison cap and pistol belt; then, remembering, he hung the pistol on the wall. He was under arrest, so he could not carry arms.

* * * *

He stepped outside and cut across the parade ground, heading for the third square brick house in the row of married officers' homes opposite. As he approached Abe Byas's house, he wondered whether he should tell Abe of Rush's revelation. He decided against it; Abe was Ervien's adjutant, honor bound to be loyal to him, and there was no use troubling Abe until he had proof.

Byas, bareheaded, was waiting on his walk when Burke crossed the drive.

"Look," Abe said mildly in greeting. "I'm adjutant of this post. You want to appear before me tomorrow morning for disciplinary action?"

Burke hauled up. "What for?"

Abe pointed to the parade ground. "It's seeded," he said carefully, distinctly. "Stay off it, will you?"

Burke grinned. "I forgot."

As they went up the walk, Abe looked reprovingly at him. "Well, you did it up brown, didn't you?"

"Didn't I?" Burke murmured.

"You'll learn," Abe said. "Just keep chewing his ears until you're in real trouble."

Burke didn't reply, and Abe mounted the steps. His house was a square brick affair with a small porch and an iron-railed widow's walk surmounting its sloping roof. Abe went in first and waved his hand toward the parlor. "Sit down. I'll get Calla."

He went on through the hall toward the back rooms.

Burke looked around the pleasant parlor, whose contents had been freighted half a thousand miles. Through the open window he caught the brassy, saucy sound of mess call being sounded, and he wondered gloomily what he was going to say to Calla.

Sighing, he turned from the window just in time to see Calla, apron over her dress, come into the room. She didn't, pause, didn't speak, only came into his arms and kissed him. After she had kissed him twice more, she hugged him and said into his ear in a low, shaky voice, "I've got to get used to missing you, Burke."

Burke smiled faintly and held her from him, looking hungrily at her. The grave and mischievous amber eyes told him nothing except that she was glad to see him. Her wide mouth, soft and smiling, was happy enough. She had been fussing with her thick golden hair: it was done differently atop her head, and he thought it beautiful, just as, without knowing why, he thought her gray dress, through the sleeves of which he could feel the rounded softness of her arms, delightful.

He said, "If that's what they call a soldier's welcome I'm for it."

He held her to him a moment, then asked, "Did Abe tell you, Calla?"

She drew back and looked gravely at him. "About your arrest? Yes, I'd have hated you forever if you'd taken your troop out as Ervien ordered." She frowned quizzically. "Did you really think I'd mind?"

"Well," Burke said slowly, "I wouldn't blame a girl for being a little mad over a postponed wedding."

Calla said, alarm in her eyes, "Who said it was postponed?"

"Look, honey," Burke murmured. "You can't marry an officer when he's under arrest. I couldn't even wear a sword at the ceremony."

"Do you think I care anything about a silly sword?" Calla flared.

"I do," Burke said grimly. "I want to know whether you'd be marrying a soldier or a civilian. So do you."

Calla sighed in mock exasperation, took his hand and led him over to the sofa and pulled him down beside her. "Burke, let's be practical. If you hadn't sassed Captain Ervien, you'd be on patrol tomorrow, wouldn't you?"

"I suppose," Burke admitted.

"Then, for heaven's sake, you're here now. You will be until the trial. It's the only chance he'll give us to be together. To hell with your arrest!"

Burke looked faintly shocked, and Calla said swiftly, vehemently, "I mean it, Burke. I'm tired of being Mrs. Hanna-to-be! The chapel is on post limits. We can get married tomorrow. In private or public, I don't care. It's nobody's business but ours."

She smiled now at her own vehemence. "Speak up, soldier."

Burke grinned. "I kind of like the idea," he murmured. "Of course—" He paused. He had just caught sight of Abe standing in the doorway. Burke said, "You've got a wife. Let me get one, will you?"

"Later," Abe said calmly. "There's a trooper at the back door. He wants to speak to you."

Burke swore under his breath and started for the door. He came back, leaned over and kissed Calla, and then went into the hall toward the kitchen. That's how much you know about the girl you'll marry, he thought wonderingly.

CHAPTER THREE

REAL TROUBLE

Lucy Byas, an older, smaller, and more placid version of Calla, was in the kitchen. She looked over her shoulder at Burke's entrance and said, "Hello, you wild-eyed Mick." Although she had a dish in each hand, Burke hugged her in passing, and then went on to the back door.

"Hello, Carney," he said to the beardless trooper on the steps, and then he saw the restrained excitement in the soldier's face. "What's the trouble?"

"I thought the lieutenant ought to know, sir. Raines and O'Mara are buildin' up a fight over issue of mounts down at the corral."

Burke scowled. "I left Raines in the hospital."

"He's on crutches, sir. Dr. Ford let him out."

Burke swore and went down the steps. "You go along to supper, Carney. And thanks." He strode down the alley, cut left down the short Street lined with the homes of the married enlisted men, and at a trot, passed A stable. Raines, K Troop's first sergeant, was a tough, tobacco-chewing bantam of a man with an aggressive loyalty to his officers, his men, and his horses. And when Burke thought to him fighting with O'Mara, the squadron bully, the sly, toadying Irishman whom anyone but Ervien would have broken and kept broken, he was worried. And Raines was on crutches.

Passing B stable at a run, he saw the place was deserted; all the troopers were at supper call. He cut in through the forage shed that lay between B stable and the corrals and saw a big supply wagon blocking the far door.

Ducking round it, he hauled up. There, in front of the corral gate in the slanting sunlight, were O'Mara and Raines. Raines, on his bandaged feet, had backed against the corral poles beside a stack of forks and shovels, and was swinging his remaining crutch in a half circle, trying to fend off the squat, long-armed O'Mara. Even as Burke saw this, O'Mara moved inside the arc of the crutch, and smashed savagely at Raines's seamed face with the swift pawing motion of a bear striking. Moving in, and pulling Raines to him, he stamped on Raines's bandaged feet; then, half turning, he picked up the smaller man, whose fists were flailing at his bearded face, and slammed him to the ground and fell on top of him.

Burke vaulted the wagon's tongue; his foot caught in one of the loops of a long stay chain festooned on the tongue, and he fell heavily and came up again, running. He saw O'Mara's fists driving into Raines's face. Burke pulled up.

"O'Mara!" he said in an iron voice. "Get up!"

The voice of authority startled O'Mara, and he was already rising when he saw that it was Burke beside him. He paused, his knees half flexed, and then slowly sank back on Raines.

"Lieutenant, you're under arrest, with no authority for anything," he said gently.

"Get to your quarters!" Burke said.

O'Mara stared quietly at him with his small red-rimmed eyes, which were calculating and sly and arrogant, and then he said in his strangely gentle voice, "Off with you, Lieutenant. I've this to finish." And he slashed savagely at Raines's face.

Burke hit him, then, in the face, a driving blow that knocked him off Raines and into the dust on his back. O'Mara sat up, raised a thick and meaty hand to his jaw, and said mildly, wickedly, "You struck an enlisted man, Lieutenant."

"Get to your quarters, O'Mara," Burke repeated. O'Mara came to his feet with a slow, sure indolence, and Burke saw that his massive shoulders had burst the seam of his blue shirt. No fear and no respect, only a kind of animal cunning was in his eyes now; he rubbed his beard gently with the back of his hand and said, "It'd be a fine thing to smash you, Lieutenant—you under arrest, and not allowed to order me. It'd be your word against mine."

"I wouldn't try it," Burke advised.

O'Mara looked around the lot in one swift glance to make sure there were no witnesses, and in that moment Burke knew that O'Mara's hatred of authority and the whole officer system, plus his sharing Ervien's dislike of K Troop, would drive him to attacking. And he would not be penalized for it.

O'Mara glanced at Raines, then moved over and kicked him in the temple. "No help there, Lieutenant," he said. Then, in a crouch, thick arms outthrust, he came slowly at Burke. He came out of his crouch like a spring uncoiling, and Burke hit him once in the throat before O'Mara's massive arms wrapped around him, squeezing him with a breath-stopping strength.

Burke felt his chest constricting, and felt O'Mara's wiry beard pricking through his blouse against his shoulder. Now O'Mara heaved to lift him off the ground, and Burke brought his knee up into O'Mara's groin with a murderous violence. O'Mara whined, his grip loosened, and Burke turned sideways, jamming the point of his shoulder into O'Mara's face. O'Mara's hold broke and, off balance, he back stepped until he crashed into the corral fence and fell heavily on his side among the clutter of stable tools. Burke was breathing deeply, impressed now by O'Mara's great strength, and wary of it.

O'Mara raised himself on an elbow and pawed the blood away from his nose. His movement stirred the tangle of tools. Looking wickedly at Burke, he pawed among them until he found a wide-tined pitchfork. Supporting himself with it, he came unsteadily to his feet, and Burke, knowing intent to murder when he saw it, reached for his pistol. He was not wearing it, he remembered then, and in the same moment, he began to back slowly away.

O'Mara lifted the fork like a spear and came shuffling toward him. Burke wheeled, looking for a weapon. Across the lot, he spied the stay chain on the wagon tongue that had tripped him. He turned and ran for it, and O'Mara ran too.

As Burke neared the wagon, O'Mara raised the fork over his head and hurled it like a spear. Burke fell and rolled under the wagon tongue, and the fork drove into the double tree, then boomed into the wagon box.

O'Mara was charging again now, and Burke, on his knees, unhooked the heavy stay chain. As O'Mara was on him, Burke slashed backhanded at him with a short length of the chain. The murderous weight of it raked across O'Mara's chest, tearing the shirt away and leaving a bloody furrow in the matted hair.

The force of O'Mara's charge was halted; he staggered back one step, caught his balance, and lunged too close. Burke, who had risen, backed up a step and raised the chain and savagely slashed it down across O'Mara's shoulders. O'Mara sank to his knees, but even then he groped out and his bloody fist gripped Burke's ankle. Again Burke brought the chain down, this time across O'Mara's black, round skull.

O'Mara fell on his face, not stirring. Burke stood over him a long minute, breathing deeply, and he thought he had killed the man and did not care.

Stepping around O'Mara, he went over to Raines, who was lying on his back as O'Mara had left him. A livid bruise was rising on Raines's temple, and the gentle slapping Burke gave his face would not bring his eyes open.

Burke picked him up, turned, and tramped through B stable. Between B and A stables, he met two troopers, and called them to him.

"Take Raines to the hospital. Then one of you go over to the officers' mess and get Dr. Ford."

Soberly, the troopers took Raines and disappeared behind A stable. Burke stood a moment brushing the dust from his uniform. He was thinking, This is real trouble, now.

There was nothing to do except report it, he knew. He turned wearily up toward the parade ground.

He had passed the barracks and was nearing the sutler's post which housed the officers' club when he saw Captain Ervien leave headquarters building and turn toward him. Burke met him in front of the post trader's.

Burke saluted. "Sir," he began formally, "I think I've probably killed your sergeant major."

Ervien's mouth opened slowly, but no words came.

Burke went on, "O'Mara was roughing up Sergeant Raines. When I ordered him to stop, he refused, saying I had no authority to issue orders. I hit him to keep him from hurting Raines. He thought that gave him the right to attach me, and he did. I think," he finished, "I may have killed him."

Burke saw the wicked anger mount in Ervien's dark eyes. "Mister Hanna, you seem to get in trouble even when confined to the post," he said in a dry and savagely formal voice. "Confine yourself to quarters and mess until I have the particulars."

"Yes, sir," Burke said, and Captain Ervien brushed past him.

Back in quarters, Burke paused long enough to send the orderly over to Byas's to explain his absence, and then went on to his room. Abe, he reflected wryly, would probably be pulled away from his supper to investigate, since he was adjutant.

He sank wearily down on his bed. He wondered idly what Raines and O'Mara had quarreled about, and then turned to his own predicament. Outside of having to face the very serious charge of striking an enlisted man, there was Calla to think about now. Even Calla, badly as she wanted them married, couldn't be married in the lounge of bachelor officers' quarters. Burke swore under his breath when he thought of it.

An orderly came from Byas's with a tray of food—the supper Burke was to have eaten with Calla and Abe and Lucy, and he ate hungrily. Afterward he loaded a pipe and lay down again and stared gloomily at the ceiling in the lowering dusk. Either he could broodingly count his sins, or what were called his sins, or he could forget them; there was no changing anything now. He swung his feet to the floor and rose and prowled restlessly to the window and came back. There, lying on the corner of his desk and covered with five weeks' dust, was his black notebook. A hundred hours of friendly argument with his fellow officers about cavalry tactics and Army practice had led him long ago to fortify and clarify his views by writing them down.

He opened the book, then closed it with disgust. What did it matter if he contended, against cavalry practice, that a mounted charge against hostile Indians was not impossible? Or that a native pony that lived off the land was often a better mount than a grain-fed Army horse?

He saw that it was getting dark, and lighted his desk lamp. He was adjusting the wick when the soft knock came on his door.

It opened immediately, and Rush Doll stepped in. Rush put his shoulder against the wall.

"You confined to quarters, like they say?"

Burke nodded.

"How's O'Mara? Have you heard?"

"All right You can't kill a brute like that. He's in the hospital. Raines is all right. He's left."

"Hear what they fought about?"

"O'Mara was tryin' to work off his crowbait mounts on K Troop replacements, and Raines wouldn't take 'em." Rush straightened up. "Well, I better go send Ponce back."

"He's there?"

Rush nodded. Burke stood hesitant a moment. He was on his honor as an officer and gentleman not to break arrest. But if he didn't see

Ponce and somehow persuade him to patience until Ervien could be convinced of the necessity for making Corinne feed his people, then he would be criminally liable.

He came to his reckless decision. "Hold him there, Rush. I'll meet you at full dark."

CHAPTER FOUR

DESPERATE RISKS

Burke couldn't take the chance that the sentry wouldn't know of his being confined to quarters, so he waited until the man had passed, then climbed out of his window. Quietly, he walked ahead until he was in the friendly shadow of the laundry. Once there, he turned and skirted the sutler's post, the barracks, and A stable, and cut down toward the blacksmith shop, which marked post limits.

A pair of troopers were doing some work there by lantern light on a wagon wheel. The near-by stable guard, carbine slacked under his arm, was peering off in the darkness. Beyond, in the half light of the lanterns, Burke could see Rush Doll and Ponce.

Burke approached the guard and returned his salute. "Bellows, I'm under arrest, you know," he began.

"Yes, sir. I heard it, sir."

Burke pointed to Doll and Ponce in the darkness. "I have to talk with that 'Pache. He's not allowed on the post after dark and I'm not allowed off it. Suppose we meet on the line and you watch us."

Bellows grinned. "As long as nobody crosses, I'm obeying orders, sir."

* * * *

Burke went on, and paused at the line of the blacksmith shop's wall. Rush and Ponce came to meet him, and in the dim light of the lantern Burke looked searchingly at Ponce. He was taller than the average Apache, perhaps thirty-eight, with squarish flat features holding a subtle blending of fierceness, pride, and cunning that had made him Tana's subchief—and a rebel. He was dressed in a dirty blue calico shirt, worn tails out, breech-clout and high leggings and moccasins. Gravely he extended his hand to Burke and shook hands.

This was hardly the time for ceremony, Burke knew, but he offered Ponce a cigar from his pocket, and it was accepted and-lighted. Burke and Rush knelt while Ponce squatted silently in the dim light. He spoke now in Apache to Rush, who interpreted to Burke.

"He says he's sorry you got in trouble for giving him and his band food," said Rush.

"Tell him I'm his friend," Burke said. "My friends don't go hungry."

Rush interpreted and Ponce answered quickly, almost with hate. Rush said dryly to Burke, "He asks if you're still his friend, because he's hungry and so are his people. They've been hungry since you sent them back."

"Ask if he hasn't been included on weekly ration issue, along with the others."

Rush and Ponce conversed a moment, and then Rush said, "He says Corinne is punishing him for breaking out last time. They receive short rations, not as much as the others. From lack of meat they're getting weak and sick. It's hard to hold the young bucks in, he says, and he wants to know how to get more meat. They've started killing their ponies, he says—and he's lying on that point, of course."

"Don't they get beef?"

Rush spoke again to Ponce, was again answered sharply, and Rush looked at Burke, irony in his eyes. "Sick beef, starved beef, with no meat on their bones."

Burke said, "Tell him I'll talk to Corinne."

Rush passed on this information, and again he received a quick and flat reply. "Tomorrow," Rush repeated, "is issue day for beef. He has told his young men to wait, to see what tomorrow brings. If they get the same sick scrub beef, Ponce says he isn't sure if he can hold them in." Rush paused. "He's threatening you, Burke. Those young men of his are pretty handy to put the blame on. He's mad, and he's threatened old Chief Tana that he'll break if his people aren't fed better."

Burke said slowly, "Tell him if he breaks, I'll hunt him down, and this time I'll kill him and every man that breaks with him."

Rush hesitated a moment before translating. When he had, Ponce gazed levelly at Burke. There was a challenge in the look and Burke's eyes met it steadily. Finally, Ponce spoke briefly, and Rush translated.

"He says you can't hunt him down. You're under arrest. The rest of the soldiers he's not afraid of."

Burke rose, signifying the end of the parley. He waited for the customary "Enju" from Ponce, which signified "All is good," but it did not come. Ponce shook hands gravely, turned, and vanished noiselessly into the night.

"He's already made up his mind to break," Burke said slowly.

Rush cursed viciously. "That damn Corinne!"

Burke stared out into the warm star-studded night. He would go to Ervien now and tell him what Ponce said, pointing out that Corinne's weekly short-weight swindle tomorrow would touch off the explosion. But Ervien would either reprimand him for not minding the Army's business, or deny that Corinne was engaged in sharp practice. Only by being confronted with the evidence of Corinne's crookedness could Burke drive him into correcting it in time.

* * * *

Reluctantly, he knew what he must do. It would have to be done without Rush, for he could not risk dragging Rush into a scheme which, if it were discovered, might cost him his livelihood. And Rush would hate him for what he would say now.

"All I can do is warn Ervien." Burke spoke resignedly. "That won't do it, Burke!" Rush said vehemently.

Burke shrugged.

There was bitterness in Rush's eyes as he said curtly, "I suppose you're right. The hell with it. Good night."

He turned stiffly and walked off toward the distant lights of the agency a half mile to the south across the flat. Burke strolled back to the deep shadow of A stable and then hauled up. He knew that what he was about to do would have far graver consequences than anything he had done thus far, and for a moment, watching the stable guard on his round, listening to the night noises of the post, he reckoned the risk and knew he must take it.

Presently, a couple of troopers joined the two already at the blacksmith shop. There was a parley there which Bellows, on his round, paused to join.

This was the chance Burke had been waiting for. Circling far outside the light of the shop lanterns, he noiselessly crossed the post limits and set out toward the agency lights. He was going to see for himself if the agency scales were rigged, as both Rush and Ponce said they were.

Once in the shelter of the agency's adobe stables, he halted and listened. He could hear the occasional bawling of restive cattle in the corral ahead. Probably hungry, he thought, and he wondered if Corinne had put out a night guard. He'd have to take that chance. From watching past issues, he knew where the scales were. An issue chute was set up leading across the scales from the corral and it was here that each Apache head of family or clan leader presented his ration ticket, had it stamped, watched his beef weighed, and received it.

A pack of dogs around the distant Apache wickiups started a fight. Under cover of their yammering, Burke made his way in the deep blackness toward the big holding corral. Once there, he moved to his right until he saw the high oblong box housing the scale machinery outlined against the sky among the chute rails.

Approaching it, he knelt and felt along its board panels for the handle of the door that gave access to the adjusting mechanism. His hand touched a hasp and then a heavy padlock. Corinne, evidently, wasn't taking chances.

Burke rose, cursing, and started beating about for a piece of iron with which to pry off the padlock. His boot hit something and he leaned down, and as he did so he heard the hoofbeats of horses at a run.

Rising, he looked off toward the dark stables, and at that moment he heard a sharp command given. "Spread out and cover the corral, men!" The voice was Ervien's.

Burke knelt, listening to the mounted troopers beating toward him. Then he turned and ran, hugging the corral fence, but the troopers fanned out quickly in the darkness, cutting off his escape. Halting, he saw a pair of troopers now rounding the end of the stables, and each held a lantern.

Burke debated vaulting the corral and hiding on the other side, but he knew his presence there would spook the wild range cattle inside. Either they would attack him, or give away his presence by their actions.

Kneeling there, a gray despair touched him, and he thought, *He knew where to come for me.* Ahead of him a trooper had turned his horse and was carefully scouting the base of the corral. The troopers with lanterns had split now, one going to either side of the corral. Ervien had halted midway between the corral and the stables.

Burke waited with a kind of fatalism, and when the trooper with the lantern approached, Burke stood up and said, "All right."

"Here he is, Captain!" the trooper called.

Burke waited, blinking against the lantern light, as the platoon collected. Ervien rode up slowly and reined in.

"You knew where to hunt for me, didn't you, Phil?" Burke said recklessly.

Ervien said coldly, "Mister Hanna, I went to your room and found you had broken arrest. Consider yourself a prisoner."

Burke said, forgetting caution, "Dismount three of your smallest men and weigh them together on that scale, Phil. See if they don't weigh over six hundred. Are you afraid to?"

"You have broken your word of honor as an officer, Mister Hanna." Ervien's voice was shaking with rage. "Now come along, or we'll bind you and carry you!"

"Sure." Burke knew he was beaten. He began to walk toward the stables, and the troopers, at Ervien's orders, flanked him. Ervien silently rode on the right flank.

They went on past the stables, between the agency buildings, and turned into the road that ran in front of Corinne's store to the post.

A brace of carriage lamps lighted the store's deep veranda, and Burke saw Corinne, soft, gray, and formless in his baggy black suit, watching silently at the top of the steps. A scattering of Apaches and agency employees were seated on the veranda benches.

As they drew even with the steps, Burke halted and looked balefully up at Corinne. Ervien, sensing trouble, said, "Forward, Mr. Hanna!"

Burke didn't move. He raised his arm now and pointed at Corinne and said slowly, "Corinne, if you short-weight that beef you issue to Ponce tomorrow, he'll break. He told me so tonight. And every drop of blood it takes to get him back here will be on your head!"

"Forward!" Ervien roared. "Sergeant, put a carbine on that prisoner and if he refuses to move shoot him!"

Burke had never ceased looking at Corinne, who did not move. Now he looked over at Ervien. "You heard it, too. I'll go now."

Burke tramped on. The troopers flanking him were quiet, awed by the gravity of their errand. Later, at the sentry gate, the sentry silently presented arms, and afterward Burke tasted the full measure of this calculated humiliation. He was an officer being brought back afoot by the commanding officer and guard, a prisoner who had broken arrest.

They filed past the sutler's post where loitering enlisted men, baffled and wondering, watched them in silence.

It was here, at the corner of the parade ground, that Ervien at last spoke and a score of men heard him. "Sergeant, put him in the guard-house, and double your guard."

CHAPTER FIVE

SURPRISE MANEUVER

Sometime after ten o'clock next morning, Burke, fed and rested, was lying on his bunk trying to pick out the separate sounds of a post working through a July morning. His barred cell was a big one, occupying half the small adobe building that lay between the two barracks. A pair of troopers were sleeping a drunk off in the cell opposite.

He turned his head at a sound in the passageway and saw Abe Byas being let in by the sergeant of the guard.

Burke swung his feet to the floor, and Abe, closing the cell door behind him, said, "Hello, Burke," with a morose lack of enthusiasm. He put his huge bulk gently on the foot of Burke's cot, regarded Burke a moment, then shook his head. "Since the middle of supper last night," he said, "I've been looking around for the pieces of all the regulations you've broken. Did you miss one?"

Burke's long face broke in a grin, and Abe regarded him unsmilingly. "Ervien has me drawing up the list of additional charges this morning."

"I added some," Burke murmured.

"For God's sake, why did you have to break arrest? Why were you at the agency?"

Burke said dryly, "I'm a kind soul, Abe. I got to wondering if Corinne watered his beef."

"Damn it, can't you be serious?"

"I am serious," Burke said gravely. "Either I'm out of the Army or he's out, after the court martial. Let's let it go at that." He wasn't going to tell Abe of his certain belief that Ervien was winking at Corinne's cheating the Apaches. Abe would be torn between his loyalty to him and his duty to Ervien and, if he became involved, would have to risk his career.

"How is Calla?" Burke asked.

"She's crazy," Abe growled. "I mean she isn't even worried."

"When'll the court martial sit, Abe?" asked Burke.

"In two weeks maybe. When I've heard all the witnesses the case will be forwarded." He rose and looked down at Burke, puzzlement in his face. "I hope you know what you're doing."

"I do. Thanks."

When Abe was gone, Burke lay down again, and he found himself thinking of the coming court martial. He had only to plead justification and state his case, but that case must be proved. He saw now that he must do two things: he must prove his charge of crookedness against Corinne, and he must prove that Phil Ervien knew of Corinne's swindle and was abetting it. *If I can't I'm cashiered,* he concluded bleakly.

* * * *

Some time later he was roused again by the sergeant's footsteps. He looked up. Calla, a covered tray in her hands, was standing by the cell door. He rose, and Calla came in. Before she put the tray down, she kissed him. "Happy wedding day," Burke said gravely.

"You wait," Calla said, merriment in her eyes. "You can't dodge it by going to jail."

Burke grinned. "Why did they let you in here?"

"I asked permission of your Captain Ervien," Calla said, and added slyly, "He's a charming man, really."

She was wearing a flowered green dress, cool and fresh as new grass, and Burke didn't wonder at Ervien's gallantry. He put the tray on the floor and pulled her down beside him, and she half turned to him, regarding him levelly and soberly.

"How much of what Abe says they say you did, did you do?"

"All of it."

"Can you justify it?"

"All of it," Burke repeated. "Either I don't belong in the Army or he doesn't, Calla."

She reached for his hand and Burke knew that she believed in him completely.

"Calla, how much of the money I gave you for our house stuff have you got left?"

"Three hundred dollars or so. Why?"

"I'm going to buy us a wedding present," Burke said musingly.

"A couple of ugly, brindle, half-starved cows." He smiled at her look of puzzlement, and then, speaking in a low voice, he told of what had happened last night, and why. He held back nothing, and finished by saying, "I never saw the scales, Calla. I can't prove anything on Corinne—and I've got to."

Calla nodded. "But what have two cows got to do with it?"

"You get our money and take it to Rush Doll. The beef issue is going on right now. Tell Rush to pick out a couple of Corinne's issue beeves—cows that are marked or disfigured, so if a man saw them once he'd never forget them. Tell Rush to buy or trade for them with the Apache who was issued them—and that Apache must be a member of Ponce's band. Does it all make sense?"

"Yes," Calla said quickly. "Either Corinne fixes the scales and weighs Ponce's beef right, or he short-weights him—and you have the evidence. If Ponce breaks, you can prove why. Oh, Burke, he won't break, will he?"

Burke shrugged. Calla stood up quickly. "I'll go now, Burke. I don't know if I can come again."

* * * *

Early that evening, the sergeant of the guard gave him a note. It contained one word, Enju, and was unsigned, and Burke knew Rush had succeeded.

He got to sleep late. At 4:30 next morning, at bare dawn, the bugle woke him. It was sounding Call to Arms.

Burke lay hearing the sound of men running and their talking. Ten minutes later, the sergeant of the guard poked his head in and said, "Thought you'd want to know, sir. Ponce's busted loose again."

Burke sank back on his cot. So it happened, just as he had warned Ervien it would. A hot anger flooded through him; men would die, ranches would be ravaged and burned, and a whole countryside thrown into terror until Ponce was brought in again. And this time, Ponce would fight. He had trusted the white man's word, and been betrayed. And the blame for all of it was on Corinne's head.

The trooper who brought Burke's breakfast told him that Ponce had killed an agency policeman in his break. The trooper didn't know how many bucks had broken with him, but they were headed west for the Tonto Rim.

Burke was almost through his breakfast when the corridor door opened and Captain Ervien, followed by Lieutenant Byas, stood aside to let the sergeant unlock his cell.

Burke put his tray on the floor and came to attention. Ervien looked haggard and worried. He said stiffly, "At ease, Mister Hanna."

Burke relaxed, glancing at Abe's sober face.

"Mister Hanna," Ervien began, "I have come to a decision I think is a fair one, and I have disregarded my personal feelings in the matter."

Burke said nothing, and Ervien said, "I am releasing you from arrest. You are to assume command of K Troop immediately and prepare to take the field."

"What's the reason, sir?"

"You are our most experienced commander in the field," Ervien said. "You know Ponce and you know how he fights. You've campaigned longer and more ably than any man in the squadron. You are needed." He added stiffly, "It is your privilege to refuse, of course. It will not influence your record. Neither," he said bluntly, will your acceptance."

"I'll accept, of course," Burke said promptly.

"Very well. Assembly will be sounded in half an hour. Have your troop ready."

Ervien went out, and Burke stared unbelievingly at Byas. "What's behind it, Abe?"

"Nothing. He said it all. We need you."

CHAPTER SIX

PLAN OF ATTACK

It was midday of the second day out of Fort Akin when Burke, topping the Tonto Rim, led K Troop in a circle and ordered dismount. Abe Byas, who had turned over his I Troop to his second lieutenant in order to join Burke's advance party, stepped heavily out of the saddle and sought the closest shade. The troopers eased from their saddles and loosened cinches that had been tightened for the long ascent, then found shelter from the blasting midday sun under the pines that grew almost to the edge of the Rim.

Burke loosened his cinch and, seeing Abe was flat on his back in the shade, moved over to Abe's horse and loosened that cinch also. A faint excitement was running through him now. Last night, Nick Arno, the chief of the scouts, had climbed close enough to the top of the Rim here to see Ponce's campfires. Ponce would know that, and would make his stand sometime today. Burke thought he knew where it would be, and he impatiently waited word from Nick, whose scouts were well to the front and flanks.

Byas said dreamily, "It's hell to carry as much weight as I do, Burke."

"It's hell on your horse, too," Burke gibed, and walked back to the edge of the Rim, passing among the resting blue-shirted troopers. At his call for volunteers from K Troop, every man passed by Surgeon Ford as able to sit in a saddle had come forward, and now he looked at them, along with his few replacements, trying to gauge their temper. They were silent, preoccupied. Having just come off the grinding patrol of sending Ponce back to the reservation, they had a personal interest in finishing the job now, Burke knew. Sergeant Raines was cruising silently by himself among the troopers, his campaign hat turned up at the back and in the front, his tight, leathery face pouched in the right cheek by his ever-present cud of tobacco. He had borrowed a pair of oversize boots to accommodate his bandaged feet, and Burke knew he felt ridiculous and therefore touchy.

At the Rim, Burke halted. A thousand feet or more below him perhaps two miles away on the backtrail, Troops I, L, and M, comprising two hundred men, toiled antlike up the first lift of the trail. Behind them a string of crawling black beads told him Rush Doll's mule-pack train was coming along. For a moment, the panorama of the Basin caught and held his attention. He had seen it many times from this point, but never twice alike. Now it was gray, stippled with green and brown, with great pools of black cloud shadow moving majestically across it like lakes of cooling lava. An almost unbearably hot draft of wind lifted ceaselessly over the Rim.

"Lieutenant, sir."

That was Raines. Burke turned and saw Nick Arno, the young half-breed Apache who was chief of scouts, trotting silently through the resting troop. From the waist up, Nick was dressed like a white man, wearing a dun calico shirt, neckerchief and black campaign hat. From the waist down, he was Apache, with breech clout, high leggings, and moccasins. The cast of his broad features was Apache, but his pale coffee-colored skin bespoke white blood.

He hauled up before Burke. "He's gettin' ready to fight, Burke," he said. "He's run far enough."

"The far bank of Quartermaster Creek?" Burke asked. This was his hunch, and he saw it confirmed by Nick's nod. "How many?"

"Sixty or seventy, not counting women and kids. They're holed up in rocks on both sides of the trail."

Burke looked beyond the resting troopers and up the timbered trail to the country ahead. The trail, he remembered, climbed over the near ridge he could see, sloped down and crossed an open park to climb again for a higher ridge before it dived steeply into the wide and sandy waterless wash that was Quartermaster Creek. It was on the far bank of the creek, among the vaulting boulders, that Ponce had forted up.

"Don't cross the creek, Nick," he said. "Scatter your boys to the right of the trail along the ridge and open up on them. Hold them there, and when you're set, start back and I'll meet you on the trail."

Nick nodded and swung into an easy trot up the trail. Burke went over to Raines.

"Raines, you ride," Burke said. "The rest of us will walk. No smoking, no talking. Ponce is about three miles ahead. Let's get going."

With Byas silently plodding behind him, Burke led the file through the timber to the ridge and over it. The humus of pine needles silenced the footfalls of the horses, and there was only the hushed sound of creaking leather. On the downslope, as the timber thinned, Burke saw the open grassy park he had promised Ervien would make a suitable assembly point, lying still and deserted in the sun.

Once there, Burke almost absently gave the command to fall out while he studied the park. His glance passed over and then returned to the left of the trail at the far edge of the timber.

Byas, from beside him, was studying the park too. He said, "I feel awful naked here, Burke. I keep thinking I see Indians behind trees."

Burke only grinned and beckoned Raines over to him. He told him to take Callahan and see if they could make their way, mounted, down the wash. "I want to know if we can get through there, mounted, to Quartermaster Creek without being seen. If there's been anybody down it ahead of you, pull back and we'll forget it."

Raines called to Callahan, and the two set out.

As Burke mounted, Byas said, "Hell, Ponce's got that wash spotted, Burke."

Burke shook his head in negation. "If we were 'Paches, he might have, Abe, but we're only dumb soldiers. A goose-trap ambush on the far bank of the Quartermaster is good enough for us. It's worked on us before, and he thinks it'll work again." He lifted his reins, just as the sound of distant scattered fire came to them. He listened a moment, then turned to Abe and grinned, "See?" he said.

"Quartermaster Creek?"

"Far bank." He put his horse into motion, calling back over his shoulder, "Post lookouts, Abe, and take over, will you?"

He rode across the park and into the timber, and the trail climbed gently again. He felt a curious impatience to examine Ponce's position, although he already pictured it. He knew, without any cynicism, that Ervien had elected him to pull his chestnuts out of the fire, and he was willing enough to do it. For this was his chance to settle his score with Ponce, as he had promised the Apache he would.

A ten-minute ride brought him just short of the timbered crest where Nick was waiting, standing beside the trail, facing the sound of firing and listening intently.

Dismounting, Burke picketed his pony off the trail and joined Nick, who wordlessly led him angling to the right of the trail into the thinning timber of the crest. Nick crawled up behind a windfall lying across the hump of the ridge; Burke came up, hatless, and bellied down beside him.

Before them, the timber ceased almost abruptly; a field of jagged and tumbled boulders sloped easily down to the steep bank of Quartermaster Creek forty yards away. To his left, and across the wide, sandy, and waterless wash, Burke saw the trail rising steeply to vanish into the boulder field piled high and vaulting on the far bank. Behind the rocks a bare and level sage flat stretched for several hundred yards until the thick timber began again. It was among those boulders on the far bank that Ponce had placed his men on both sides of the trail, waiting contemptuously. Now Burke could pick out the sharp flat crack of Ponce's Winchesters, which were answered by the muffled, heavier bark of the scouts' cavalry carbines to his right on this bank.

Nick touched his arm and pointed across the wash to the right and rear of Ponce's position. Burke saw a column of dust lifting in a slow spiral above the pines, and he knew it was Ponce's pony herd. *He's keeping them moving in a circle,* Burke thought. *Bait for us.*

Nick said then, "Ponce thinks you're in jail, Burke. That trap is meant for the others."

Burke grunted assent. He'd forgotten that, and it would help. He told Nick to keep the scouts in position and firing, so as to make Ponce waste ammunition, adding, "If they move to our left across the trail, send back word."

Returning to his horse, Burke mounted. The rightness of the plan he had half-formed in his mind was confirmed by what he had seen. If only Raines's report was favorable. Impatient now, he lifted his horse into a canter down the trail to the assembly point.

* * * *

As he rode into the park, he saw that I, L, and M Troops had arrived and dismounted, and were scattered across the park in the hot sunshine, roughly holding formation. The officers, dismounted beyond his own K Troop in the middle of the park, were gathered in a loose circle around Ervien, who was still on his horse.

Burke rode straight for his troop. Reining in, he asked, "What luck, Raines?"

Raines shifted his tobacco before he spoke. "We got down the wash without any trouble. There's been nobody over it, Lieutenant."

"Can a troop get through unobserved?"

"In a column of troopers, yes, sir."

"Did you scout the other side?"

Raines nodded. "Yes, sir. We found a wash and went up it into the boulders."

Burke felt a quiet elation. "What's it like on top?"

"Past the boulders, it's mostly level, with sage and rabbit-brush flats clean to the timber."

"Fine work, Raines. Thank you."

"Sir," Raines said ominously, "O'Mara's along!"

"Keep away from him. We've got other business, Raines." Then he understood that this might be Raines's way of warning him. He looked levelly at the sergeant, and said, "I see. Thank you, Raines."

He rode over to join the officers. As he approached he heard Ervien say fretfully, "I still think it's unwise to move until Doll's pack train is here." He caught sight of Burke and swung out of his saddle. Without his blouse and in his shirtsleeves, Ervien seemed somehow frail, soft, and ill at ease. A day-old beard blurred the edges of his sharp face; his uniform was dusty and his shirt was staining with sweat at his belly and back. He contrived to hide his harried expression from only the closest observer as he said stiffly, "Well, Mister Hanna. You're advance party. What have you found?"

Burke swung down and looked at the ground about him. He found a bare patch of clay a yard or so to the right of him. Stepping over to it, he started to kneel, then looked up at Ervien. "You want your first sergeants to hear this, sir?" be asked.

"Very good idea," Ervien murmured.

Byas turned and shouted, "Pass the word. All sergeants assemble here!" Burke knelt and smoothed out the clay, then began to draw his map with his finger. The officers collected about him in a loose circle, and the sergeants, as they came up, fell in behind them.

Burke, waiting for the laggards, looked up to see Sergeant O'Mara, his nose swollen but his face otherwise unmarked, watching him with bland and arrogant eyes.

They were all watching now, and Burke explained his simple map, giving Ponce's position, the locations of the pony herd, and the disposition of the scouts.

When he had finished, he looked up at Ervien. He had, he saw immediately, done the wrong thing, for Ervien was looking at him with an air of expectancy mingled with relief, as if the burden of decision had been lifted from him. Now the harried expression returned to his face as he looked awkwardly about him, and saw that the other officers were watching him. He cleared his throat and said formally, "Any suggestions, Mister Hanna?"

"Yes, sir," Burke said bluntly. "It's the usual sucker's trap he's set. I propose we don't oblige him."

Lieutenant Umberhine laughed. Ervien looked reprovingly at the stocky officer and then at Hanna. "None of us want to, I assure you. Go ahead."

Burke looked over at Umberhine, now. "You laughed, Brad, and you're right. Ponce expects us to fight across the wash and make for the pony herd he's labeled for us, so he can butcher us in that wash where the trail crosses."

"What's your scheme?" Byas said.

Burke told them of Raines's reconnaissance, which offered a covered route around across the creek and behind Ponce's flank. One troop, Burke said, should reinforce the present line of scouts at the wash; a second troop should take Raines's route, while the other two troops should swing around to the right to make a demonstration against Ponce's other flank as if to cut between him and his pony herd.

"Is this a fake demonstration, Mister Hanna?" Ervien asked sharply. "You just told us Ponce expects us to do that."

"No, sir," Burke said. "That's where we ram home the first hard attack—a quarter mile to the right of the trail where the banks are lower."

"Approximately where Ponce expects us to," Ervien said dryly. "Be consistent, Mister Hanna."

"I am," Burke said flatly. "We don't ram it home until the troop that's crossed the wash and hidden on his other flank is all set and firing. When Ponce sees his pony herd threatened and moves to protect it, the hidden troop will take him from the rear and cut off his escape into the timber." He looked at the circle of attentive faces now. "With eighty men, he can't fight two ways. The two troops on the right will cross between him and his pony herd, then wheel and cut into him."

Burke rose, and Ervien knelt and studied the map. Sergeant O'Mara, behind him, leaned hands on knees and looked over his shoulder. The other officers crowded up.

After a long moment, Ervien rose. "We'll accept that, Mister Hanna. It's very good," he acknowledged. Now, regarding each officer in turn, he was once more the sharp garrison soldier. His work was done for him. To Lieutenant Umberhine he gave command of Troops L and M; they were to force the crossing on the right. Byas was to command Troop I, which was reserve, and the scouts at the trail crossing.

To Burke Hanna and K Troop fell the mission of crossing the Quartermaster unobserved and coming in behind Ponce. Burke felt a grim satisfaction at this. Ervien himself, as commanding officer, elected to take his position behind Lieutenant Umberhine's main attack.

As the group broke up to scatter for their horses, Ervien called, "Good luck, gentlemen. I will post a lookout to our right and rear."

Burke fell in beside the lumbering Byas as they sought their horses. Abe glanced fondly at him and said, "You earn your pay, don't you?"

Burke didn't answer; he said quietly, "Abe, your troop won't need pistols. I want to borrow them."

Byas said slowly, "All right, Burke. But why?"

"This is one time," Burke said grimly, "we'll get more than ponies and squaws. I'm after the bucks."

"At short range," Byas said.

"As short as I can make it," Burke murmured.

CHAPTER SEVEN

BETRAYED

As K Troop was ready to move, Burke looked across the park and saw that Ervien, with O'Mara at his side, was still studying the map, pointing to it and gesturing vehemently. Ervien, he supposed, would keep O'Mara, which was satisfactory to K Troop, he knew.

Burke let Raines and Callahan precede him into the wash, then giving K Troop the order to mount, he led on. The issue of extra pistols was causing comment, he knew, and he would give his troop the reason in good time. Soon the high clay walls closed about them, and the heat was stifling, so that when they came into the blazing brightness of Quartermaster Creek's sandy bed, it was almost a relief.

Here Raines's trail, hidden from Ponce's view by a sharp bend in the stream bed, crossed and dropped downstream a hundred yards, then headed up a wide sandy draw through the boulders that climbed steeply as it narrowed to little more than the width of a horse.

As Burke pulled out of the arroyo in one last steep climb, he saw, immediately to his right, Callahan holding his own and Raines's horses. Beyond Callahan, a long low clay dune that cut back toward the creek screened his view of Ponce's position.

Raines, his dusty blue uniform almost the color of the clay, was lying on his stomach down below the crest of the ridge, which was covered with rabbit brush and sage.

Forming his troop in line below the crest, Burke gave the command to dismount and joined Raines.

The wide sage flats lay in front of him now, separating the timber to his left from the boulder-studded canyon rim to his right. He could tell that L and M Troops had joined the engagement by the increase in the volume of fire and, watching carefully, he caught an occasional glimpse of a trooper, small in the distance across the creek, edging his way forward.

Leaving Raines in observation, Burke pulled back behind the dunes and called the troop together. His old troopers were watching him expectantly; only the volunteer replacements showed any uneasiness.

Burke began easily. "This is one time a soldier gets in the first shot with an Apache. They haven't seen us. We're going to scatter down this ridge at ten-yard intervals and fire two volleys from carbines. That lets L and M know we're in position, and it tells Ponce he's outflanked. Then you'll fall back to your mounts."

There was a puzzled silence at this last piece of information. Finally, Callahan said, "Beg pardon, sir, but these extra pistols. What are they for?"

"A mounted charge," Burke said quietly.

An even longer silence followed, and Burke saw the old troopers were mulling this over. He glanced up the ridge and saw Raines looking at him. He thought Raines was grinning, but he couldn't be sure. A mounted charge against Indians, of course, had been given up by the cavalry long ago as impossible, and Burke knew the older troopers were remembering this.

He said, "When we volley at Ponce's rear, he'll have to pull out of those rocks or die there. Once he's in the open and afoot, you'll have a horse under you, twelve shots in your pistols and five in your carbines. If you're tired of fighting Indians the way an infantryman does, here's your chance. We're going to wind this one up without a foot race."

The men laughed at that, and Burke said, "All right, move forward. Open fire when I do."

The troop scattered down the ridge, and Burke pulled his carbine from his saddle scabbard, and climbed the ridge to he down beside Raines. He surveyed the boulder field, and catching a movement there, he shot carelessly at it. A ragged volley followed; men were reluctant to shoot without targets, and the Apaches were well hidden.

The second volley, sweeping nearly the whole of Ponce's line beyond the trail, stilled Ponce's Winchesters. Then, as Burke had hoped, there was a stir of activity in the rocks. Several bucks changed positions; a handful stood up briefly, staring at the dunes. He heard angry and excited shouting, and one buck broke for the long run to the timber, then, thinking better of it, dropped behind a clump of sage.

The overtone of L and M's fire dropped off. Burke thought,

They're crossing, and lifted his glance to the bare bank of the creek. What he saw puzzled him. Blue-clad troopers were pulling out of their positions along the rocks of the creek bed, and were hastily retiring up the slope and over the crest.

* * * *

Raines, seeing it, spat, then looked quizzically at Burke and asked, "What's that for?"

Burke shook his head in wonderment. If they were reforming for a dismounted charge, they'd better hurry.

Then his attention was yanked to Ponce's band. They were drifting out of the rocks now to face this new threat to their rear. There was no concerted movement; here a naked buck, mud-smeared, bent over and running, would show himself a second and drop, and another would rise after him. The direction of their movement was obliquely across K Troop's field of fire, and Burke thought, *He's trying to get between us and his camp in the timber. If he reaches timber, he's gone.*

He said, "Come on, Raines," and turned and ran downhill for his horse, raising his arm in the signal to the waiting troopers to mount. Riding immediately to his position in front of center, he ordered, "By the right flank," and rapidly moved the troop, still hidden by the dune, toward the creek. When the lead trooper had almost reached the rocks, Burke pulled his pistol and signaled, "By the left flank."

The troop turned into line, labored up the short climb, reached the crest, and, as if heeding a signal unspoken, boiled down the far side and out onto the flats at full gallop, yelling wildly.

A hundred and fifty yards ahead was the scattering of Ponce's bucks who had broken from the boulders. At sight of the charging line of mounted troopers, they remained motionless, momentarily stunned with surprise. This was not the way they fought; nor had they ever fought mounted soldiers before. Then the panic hit them, and they milled about in confusion, firing wildly and inaccurately.

Burke rode hard for the center of the band. Holding his fire until he was almost on them, he chose a frightened young buck as his man and rode him down. The impact hurled the buck into a kneeling Apache ahead whose Winchester was already leveled at Burke. The gun went off and the Apache raised his gun as a pike and thrust savagely at Burke. With his pistol arm, Burke fended off the blow, and then he was past, and turning in his saddle, he leveled and shot almost over his horse's croup into the Apache's side.

His horse swerved, almost unseating him, as Trooper Breen, still mounted, cut across his path. Burke saw the reins of Breen's horse flying; the man had both arms folded across his belly, and was swaying drunkenly in the saddle. At the impact of Burke's horse, Breen pitched sideways and fell, and Burke's horse caromed off to the right.

Wheeling, Burke roweled his horse to complete the circle and found himself almost alone in swirling dust. The momentum of the first charge had taken the troopers past him, and now he saw the half-dozen desperate Apaches who had withstood the charge firing at the galloping troopers, some of whom had fallen. A score of downed Apaches lay scattered in the choking dust raised by the charge. Burke had already chosen the nearest Apache when he heard the terrified protesting moan of a man to his left. Burke swiveled his glance and saw two Apaches, one stripped, the other in a dirty calico shirt, savagely clubbing a downed trooper with their gun butts. Burke saw that the buck in the calico shirt was Ponce.

Burke fired, and Ponce's companion ran. Then two troopers, both mouthing the Rebel yell, cut in front of Burke, heading for the remaining Apaches, and Burke had to pull up to avoid collision. As the two riders cleared him, he saw Ponce, dropped on one knee, some thirty yards away, his Winchester slacked hesitantly in his arms. As soon as he identified Burke, he raised his gun. Instinctively, Burke flattened out on the neck of his horse. The shot came immediately, and Burke felt his horse shudder at the impact. As if propelled from a sling, Burke was catapulted over the animal's head. He landed heavily on his chest in the dust, the breath driven from him.

Gagging, he rolled on his left side so that his pistol arm was free. Ponce shot again. The noise was deafening, and Burke felt the sting of powder. He bent back his head and saw, not ten feet away, Ponce's squat figure half hidden in dust, levering a shell. Burke was lying on his side; with no time to roll on his belly, he streaked up his pistol and shot immediately at the dust-blurred outline of Ponce, which was canted awkwardly in his vision.

He thought he had missed; he rolled over, panicked, expecting Ponce's shot, but the barrel of Ponce's gun slowly tilted down, halted, was inched up again as if he were lifting a ponderous weight. The calico shirt began to stain redly at the belly. Burke shot at the stain and Ponce went over backward, fell heavily, and lay still.

Burke rose now and was immediately aware that something had happened. The close-hand fighting was over; the troopers scattered over the flats who were herding their prisoners back were now under fire themselves from the rocks and from the dunes, behind which the Apaches had filtered. Raines and a half-dozen dismounted troopers were fighting their horses quiet, and kneeling to minimize the target they presented. Even from the timber came shots from the bucks who had taken refuge there.

* * * *

Burke looked bleakly off across the creek, a hot sense of betrayal within him. Where were L and M Troops? K had been left to make the fight alone, and unless they got out of here, the tables would be completely turned on them. They were exposed now.

Burke saw one of the volunteer replacements sitting up in the dust a few yards from him, flexing a bloody arm with a look of bafflement on his young face.

Burke ran to him, helped him to his feet, and half dragged, half carried him toward Raines and the men guarding the prisoners. Lagging troopers were racing toward the same point.

Burke called sharply, "Callahan, take your squad and mount the wounded men. Raines, take the second squad and bind those prisoners. The rest of you scatter and make a run for the rocks. When you get there dismount and get into action at once."

As the troopers dispersed and rode for the boulders, enough fire was drawn off the wounded to allow Burke and Callahan to mount them. Raines left, directed by Burke to hole up close to the trail, and presently, still under inaccurate fire, Burke mounted the dead Trooper Breen's horse and headed for the rocks, bringing up the rear.

Fifty feet into the tangle of high boulders, Callahan and two troopers had already found some shade and were making the wounded men comfortable. Burke, stepping out of the saddle close by, heard his dismounted troopers firing, and he felt a savage and wicked anger at this bungling. L and M had never tried to cross.

The rocks held the blasting heat of the overhead sun. Burke took off his hat and wiped his brow with his sleeve.

Looking back over the flats, he caught occasional glimpses of running Apaches. Keeping to cover, they were rallying to attack again, knowing they could win now. These rocks, Burke knew, had won K

Troop only temporary respite; this sort of cover suited the Apaches best, and they were shrewd enough to know if they could corner this scattering of deserted troopers here, the soldiers would die. We've got to get some help, Burke thought. Damned if we'll run. I Troop must come to us. There was the trail down to the Quartermaster and across it, along which the ambush was originally laid. Was it still held by the Apaches?

After a moment he called, "Callahan!"

"Yes, sir." Callahan made the last of the wounded comfortable, then came up beside Burke.

"Callahan, we've got to get word to I Troop to cross the creek and reinforce us. The trail over there is the only way to them, and God knows what's down there."

He paused, his face set, sobered by the thought of what he had been going to ask of this man.

"You want me to try it, sir?"

"I guess not," Burke said slowly.

"I'll make it, sir. Let me try."

Somebody must go, Burke knew, and he steeled himself and said, "All right. Tell Lieutenant Byas we're clearing out both sides of the trail, and it'll be safe for him to bring I Troop across. Tell him to hurry it. Good luck."

Callahan mounted, rode out of the rocks and turned left, and was lost to sight around the boulders.

Burke now posted the two troopers among the rocks with orders to fire at will and mounted out and turned through the rocks toward the trail. He had traveled only a hundred feet or so when he found Raines and two more troopers hidden back among the rocks. Raines had their prisoners lying flat on the ground, face down, and was directing the fire of the other two troopers.

Dismounting, Burke briefly told Raines his plan, and Raines ordered the waiting troopers to go out and pull in both flanks to the edge of the trail.

When they were gone, Burke stood looking at the half-dozen naked and sweating Apaches stretched belly down on the ground. They were watching him carefully, a hot hatred in their eyes, and he knew that however this fight turned out, it would settle nothing with these people; they had a deep and abiding grudge; nourished by the actions of men like Corinne.

The sound of an approaching horse roused him, and he looked over his shoulder. There, among the boulders, stood Callahan's horse, riderless, its rump bleeding from a long gash.

Raines and Burke glanced dismally at each other, and Raines said around his tobacco, "You hold these monkeys, Lieutenant. I'll go."

Burke was touched with a gray despair. He shook his head. "No. You know what's got to be done, Raines. Hold that trail open for us. Either kill those devils guarding it or keep them down until we're through."

He got into the saddle, just as the slug from a searching shot ricocheted off a near-by boulder. Time was precious now, he knew.

CHAPTER EIGHT

JUSTICE DONE

As he rode on toward the trail, Burke put as many rocks as he could find between him and the Apaches on the flats, but the shooting was uncomfortably close.

When at last he picked up the trail, and turned into it, he saw troopers already forted up behind rocks on either side and shooting.

And then he gave his attention to what lay ahead. The trail, he remembered, twisted and turned between towering rocks, dropping steeply for fifty yards to the bed of the creek, and every rock was big enough to hide a dozen Apaches. Pulling his pistol, he urged his horse into a trot and then roweled him into a run. Then, leaning flat on his neck, he gave him his head. He was going to run through, somehow.

Rounding the first twist in the trail, Burke's knee was raked savagely against a jutting boulder, but he did not rein in. His horse stumbled once, recovered in time to hurtle around another boulder and take the steep drop in a lunge that almost unseated Burke. And then, coming around another sharp curve, he saw what he had been expecting.

Callahan lay in the trail between precipitous walls. The two Apaches cutting his already mutilated body had had no warning of Burke's presence until they looked up to find horse and rider hurtling down on them. One buck clawed at the rock in his haste to get out of the way, then turned and ran down the trail.

Burke roweled his horse savagely at the other Apache, who was flattened against the wall, drawing his knife. Burke shot him in the face, then raised his pistol at the buck running ahead, but his hammer fell on an empty chamber.

Freeing his foot from the stirrup, Burke raced his pony up close to the Apache, then kicked out solidly, catching the buck between the shoulders. The buck went down between the pony's legs and his scream was cut off sharply. Burke yanked his reins up as the buck, tangled among his pony's legs, tripped him. For a moment, Burke thought the pony would go down, but suddenly he was free and running again.

* * * *

Two more lowering curves in the trail, and Burke saw the gleaming sand of the river bed ahead. From somewhere up the rocks on the right a futile shot searched for him, and then he was in the deep sand of the wash. Under Burke's urging, the pony labored through it, as an erring marksman among the rocks kept firing swiftly and inaccurately at them.

At the far bank, Burke reined down to a walk for the climb. Pulling onto the bank, he saw Abe Byas and two troopers waiting for him behind a large protecting rock.

Burke swung out of the saddle and said shortly, "Bring your men over, Abe. And make it fast."

Byas hesitated and Burke's ragged temper flared. "Damn it, man, you're reserve and I'm calling on you

"Take it easy, Burke," Abe said. "I was wondering about the trail."

"It's cleared," Burke said. "Make it fast, Abe, or I'm all that's left of K."

Abe gave orders to his sergeant, then turned to regard Burke.

"What happened to L and M Troops?" Burke demanded angrily. "Did they ever cross?"

Byas shook his head. By now, the first of Nick's scouts were coming at a jog down the trail, and Burke halted them long enough to tell them what he wanted. The trail was being cleared by K Troop. He would lead the scouts and I Troop, dismounted, up the trail, where they would split, travel the edge of the boulder field in both directions for five hundred yards, then, flanking the Apaches, dig them out of the rocks.

Walking across the bed of Quartermaster Creek was a slogging, exhausting job, and Burke's legs were trembling with weariness when he reached the other side. Without a pause, he started up the trail, Nick ahead of him, Byas behind. Only a scattering of shots had harassed them as they crossed. There was steady fire now above them in the boulders on both sides of the trail but none of it was directed at them, and Burke knew Raines was obeying instructions to keep the

Apaches down.

Reaching the top, Burke and Byas divided the squads, two to each side of the trail, and the hunt was on. But it lasted only a matter of minutes. The reinforcing I Troopers, hunting in pairs, and pushing the Apaches from the flanks toward the center where K Troop was waiting, were too much. The Apaches were killed, or gave up, seeing the hopelessness of their position.

When the first scattering of sullen prisoners began to trickle in, Burke sought out Byas, and found him looking over the wounded men. Burke, bone-weary and exhausted and wet with sweat, was leaning up against a rock in a piece of shade when Abe approached.

"You feel like turning over the cleanup job to a junior officer, Abe?"

"All right. Why?"

"Then come with me," Burke said grimly. "Somebody's going to answer my questions."

Byas knew he was referring to L and M's disappearance.

They borrowed two horses and rode down the trail and across the river. When they reached the timbered crest on the far bank, the trail widened, and Burke reined in to let Abe come abreast of him.

"What happened, now, Abe?"

"I never made it out," Abe said wearily. "L and M started to cross after your volleys, then they were pulled back. I sent a runner to Ervien asking what was wrong. He came back with the answer that dust had been sighted to his right and rear, that he was pulling back to protect our flank, and for me to have the reserves ready to move."

Burke's baleful glance settled on him. "Did you hear any shooting back there, Abe?"

"Not a shot."

Burke was silent a moment and then murmured, "It better be so."

When the timber thinned out and they could see the park where the assembly point was, Burke saw that L and M Troops had come in only minutes before. Some of the troops were still loosening cinches. Beyond them, Rush Doll's packers were just beginning to unload the mules in the shade.

And then Burke saw Ervien. He and the officers of L and M Troops were kneeling in the sun just where he had left them over his map of the battle plan in the center of the park. Rush Doll, hands on hips, was looking over Ervien's shoulder.

Burke and Abe rode directly up to them and dismounted, and Burke saw instantly by the faces of the officers gathered around Ervien that a bitter argument had been interrupted.

* * * *

Ervien seemed shocked by Burke's dust-grimed appearance. He rose now as Burke dismounted, and said crisply, "Well, Mister Hanna, what have you to report?"

Burke said with an ominous quiet, "Ponce is dead, twenty-three of his men are dead, and the rest have surrendered. Three dead and three wounded from K Troop." He paused. "How many dead and wounded in L and M, sir?"

"Look, Burke," Lieutenant Umberhine said hotly. "I was—"

"Let your commanding officer answer, Brad," Burke murmured, watching Ervien.

Ervien's sunburned face flushed a deeper red. "I countermanded Brad's order to advance across the creek." His voice was quiet, almost arrogant, and he stood stiffly erect.

"Why, sir?"

"Abe has probably told you. The lookout I posted saw dust clouds to the rear and right of our position. I couldn't risk leaving our flanks open, so I ordered L and M back to protect our position."

"And were they hostiles, sir?" Burke asked evenly. "As it turned out, they weren't," Ervien said.

"It was me," Rush Doll drawled. "My pack mules stirred the dust."

Burke frowned. "What were you doing to the right and rear of L and M Troops, Rush?" he asked. "This was the assembly point."

"I got the order from the captain through O'Mara," Rush said slowly, looking toward Ervien.

Ervien nodded. "That's right. L and M were the bulk of the troops to be supplied. Doll could have followed our advance across the creek much easier than waiting here to move across."

"You didn't tell me that, sir," Umberhine said angrily.

Ervien looked calmly at him. "An oversight. I apologize, Brad."

Burke said slowly, "If you knew Doll was coming that route, the dust shouldn't have surprised you."

"I didn't see the dust or its position," Ervien said impatiently. "It was reported to me by the lookout."

"Let's talk to that lookout," Burke said. "Who was he?"

Ervien hesitated a split second, and then said, "Sergeant O'Mara."

Umberhine shouted for O'Mara. Burke glanced fleetingly at Byas, who was studying Ervien with a sober puzzlement in his face.

O'Mara broke away from a cluster of troopers, approached, and saluted. Ervien began, "Sergeant, tell—"

"One moment, sir," Burke said flatly. "I'm going to ask him." He looked levelly at O'Mara and the sergeant blandly returned his stare. Burke said, "You knew Doll was coming up on L and M's flank, O'Mara. Who did you think raised that dust?"

"I only reported it, sir," O'Mara said in his gentle, sly voice. "I was not asked my opinion."

"If you had been asked your opinion, what would you have said?" Burke asked dryly.

"I'd have said we should protect ourselves till we were sure."

Burke shifted his glance to Byas and said slowly, "There you are, Abe."

Ervien said sharply, "There who is, Mister Hanna? Since when are a commanding officer's orders subject to discussion?"

Burke's hot glance settled on Ervien now. "Since today, Phil. You pulled out of the fight and left K Troop to be massacred. If we didn't have the luck of the damned, the lot of us would be dead now. We aren't—thanks to I Troop." He looked at the group of officers. "Now hear me. Abe, you're adjutant and next in command. I demand you place Captain Ervien and Sergeant O'Mara under arrest for dereliction of duty."

"I demand it, too!" Umberhine said flatly. "Damned if I'll let any man make me a coward!"

Abe Byas said slowly, "I'd like it a lot better if I knew the reason for this, Burke."

"I'll give you that, too," Burke said. "Corinne has cheated the Indians blind, and Ervien has protected him. When I recommended Ervien report Corinne's dishonesty, I got sent on six months of patrol. And when Ponce broke out, Ervien knew he was in trouble, because I warned him Ponce would break." He looked around at his fellow officers. "You all saw that plan of battle I submitted. You saw where K Troop, myself commanding, was placed. If anything slipped, we were in a fair position to be wiped out. It slipped, all right—and I say Ervien, in collusion with O'Mara, planned to kill me and my troop."

"But proof, man, proof," Abe said gently.

"Of Corinne's crookedness? I've got it at the post. The rest will come out in the court martial—his or mine."

There was a long moment of silence, which was broken at last by Ervien. "Mister Hanna, you are now under arrest—again."

Abe Byas said gently, "No, Captain Ervien. It's my duty as senior officer to place you under arrest and assume command."

Ervien looked arrogantly about him. "Very well. All of you will undergo a court martial for mutiny."

* * * *

The victors of the battle of Quartermaster Creek reached Fort Akin a little after nine o'clock the second night after the battle. The post was ablaze with lights, and the veranda of the sutler's post crowded with the garrison soldiers and the womenfolk of absent men.

As the troopers were wearily scattering to their barracks five horsemen entered through the north sentry gate and rode along the parade ground to dismount at headquarters building, where lamps were lighted.

Lieutenant Byas led the way into the building, spoke to the sergeant, and went immediately into Captain Ervien's office. He spoke courteously to Mr. Corinne, who had been sitting beside Ervien's desk, then stepped aside to let Captain Ervien, Lieutenant Umberhine, Rush Doll, and Burke Hanna enter.

As Burke closed the door, Corinne said irritably, "Phil, I ought to be over checking in that pack of Ponce's scoundrels. Can't this wait?"

"No," Byas said bluntly. He walked over to the desk, sat on its edge, and glanced at Burke. "Go ahead, Burke."

Corinne's glance flicked to Burke, who was already looking at him.

"Corinne," Burke said, "Rush Doll has two cows in his corral. They were issued by you to Klin-se at Saturday's issue. Klin-se has kept his ration slip—with your figures."

He paused. Corinne looked straight ahead and said nothing. Burke went on, "We're going over and weigh them on the agency scales."

Corinne looked at Ervien, and only now did he begin to suspect something was amiss. Abe's message summoning Corinne tonight was delivered by a trusted trooper who had been told to explain nothing of what had passed at the assembly point. Corinne said dryly, "Are you the commanding officer now, Mister Hanna?"

"Lieutenant Byas is."

Corinne looked again at Ervien, and Ervien nodded.

Corinne's already flabby face seemed to sag. He looked despairingly at Burke and said, "Our scales were broken, Mister Hanna."

"Give it up, Alec." Ervien's voice was quiet, sardonic. "You're kicking him out?" he asked Byas.

"As fast as he can pack up," Abe said grimly. "What'll satisfy you completely? If I get out, too?" Byas glanced questioningly at Burke.

"Yes," Burke said implacably. "Get out. Resign or face a court martial—if Lieutenant Byas will let you. He doesn't have to."

Abe rose from the desk and indicated the chair. "Write it out."

Ervien sat down wearily and Byas strode past Burke and went out into the anteroom, leaving the door open behind him. Burke heard him say, "Sergeant, before you close up, fill out papers reducing Sergeant O'Mara to private on stable police."

When he came back, Ervien looked up from his writing. "Would you like me to give a reason?" he asked Byas.

"You've been given it," Byas said quietly. "You're no good. Officially you can say 'for the honor of the service.'"

Ervien's face flushed, and his glance dropped to the paper. He signed his name, rose, and extended the paper to Byas, who put it on the desk without looking at it.

"Get out of that uniform. Your transportation will be ready in an hour," Byas said. "We'll send your stuff to Corinne. You," he added to Corinne, "hand over your books to Lieutenant Hanna tomorrow morning at eight o'clock. Don't try to go to your office. It's under guard."

* * * *

Some minutes later, Burke and Byas said goodnight to Rush and Umberhine and wearily headed for the lights of Byas's house. Halfway across the parade ground, Burke said, "Abe."

"What?"

"I'm on your grass seed. So are you."

Abe laughed. "The hell with it. As the commanding officer, I can walk where I want."

At the house, Abe opened the door and stood aside to let Calla come into Burke's arms. Then he went past them and inside to greet his wife. Minutes later, when Burke, with Calla, came into the living-room, Abe and Lucy were standing in the middle of the room arm in arm.

Abe said, "Calla, do you want the chaplain tonight, or would you rather be married tomorrow in your own house?" I

Calla grinned. "I can wait. But where's my own house?"

"You're standing in it. I'm taking over Ervien's house tomorrow. He's resigned."

Calla looked up at Burke, then glanced at Abe. "Make it early, will you please?"

THE ORIGINAL
"ABOUT THE AUTHOR"

For sheer storytelling ability, for credible and convincing action, few other writers of Western stories can match Luke Short in registering the "feel" of the time and place. As the author of such great action novels as *Fiddlefoot, Coroner Creek, Ramrod, And the Wind Blows Free,* and *Hardcase,* Luke Short stands in the van of writers whose stories tell of the romance and violence and color of the great American West.

Although not a born Westerner, Short has lived in the Southwest for many years. Here he can soak up color and background for his stories of the West That Was, and there is no more exciting and thrilling background for tales of true adventure.

www.ingramcontent.com/pod-product-compliance
Lightning Source LLC
Chambersburg PA
CBHW050912120626
46552CB00004B/1546